PUG

by Ethan Long

I Like to Read®

Holiday House / New York

Pug sees Peg.

Pug sees Mom.

Pug sees Dad.

Yap Yap Yap Yap Yap Yap Yap

Pug sees Tad.

Tad sees Pug.

Pug wants to go.

No, Pug, no.

Go, Pug, go.

No Peg.

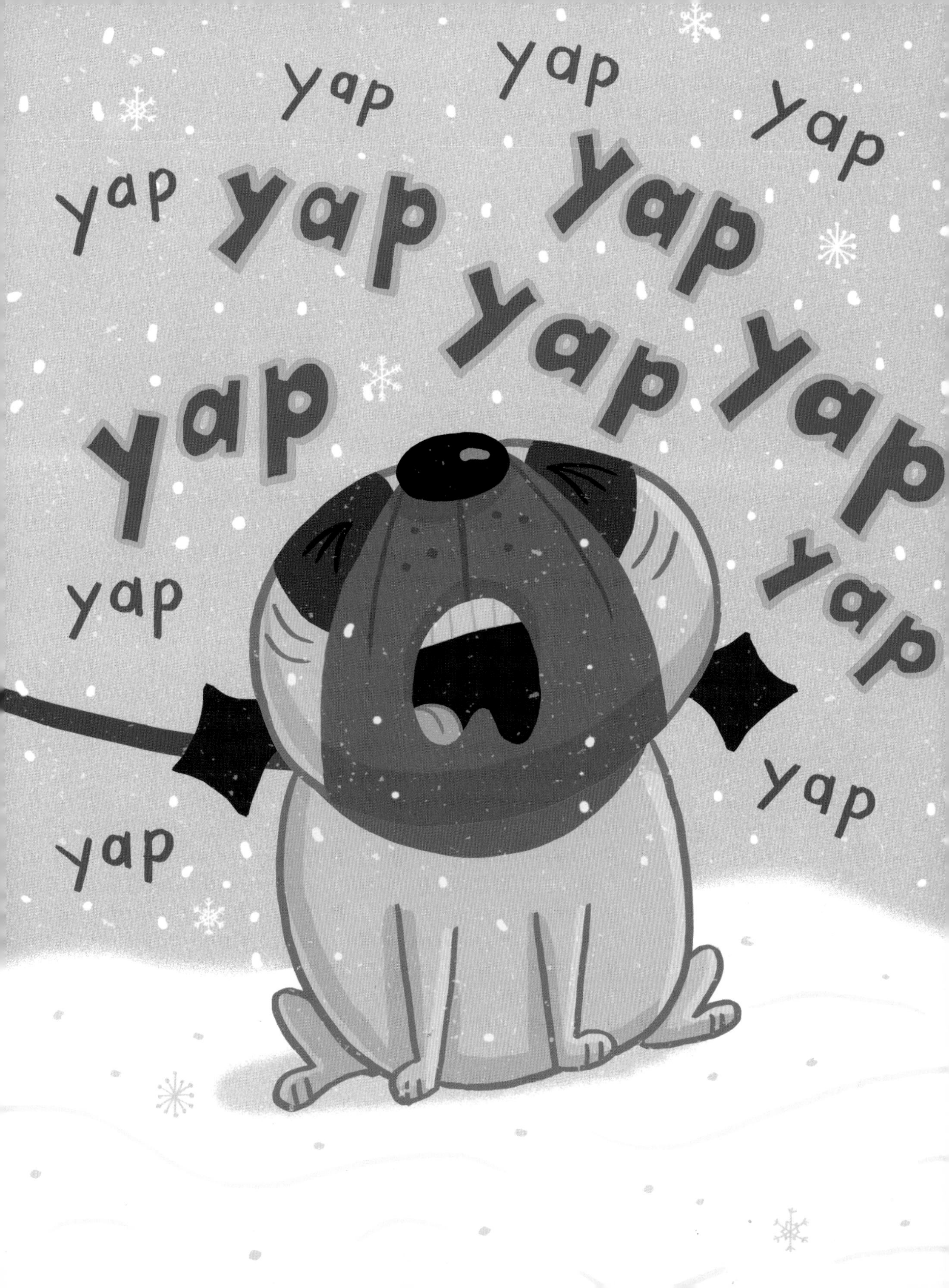
yap
yap
yap
yap
yap
yap
yap
yap
yap
yap
yap
yap
yap

Pug sees Peg.

Library of Congress Cataloging-in-Publication Data is available.

ISBN 978-0-8234-3645-3 (hardcover)

ISBN 978-0-8234-3688-0 (paperback)